Hogger
the
Hoarding Beastie

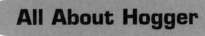

All About Hogger

Motto:	"He who has the most toys, wins!"
Hobby:	Collecting, then putting his name on toys
Dislikes:	People who won't let him go first
Favorite Food:	Stuffed eggs and succotash
Ambition:	To be an accountant
Bad Habit:	Always says, "Me first" and refuses to share his toys with others
Hero:	King Midas

Written by Kathleen Duey and Ron Berry
Illustrated by Chris Sharp
Digital Illustration by Gary Currant

1

Executive producer
John Christianson

Editorial director
Annette Norris

Digital editing
Matt Shaw

Hello, my name is Figaro.
Hogger is a friend of mine, but he's a
selfish Beastie! *I mean really selfish!*

It's Hogger's birthday and we're all
going to his house to surprise him.
Do you want to come, too?

This is Hogger's house.
Watch out for all the little signs.
Hogger makes sure everyone
knows which things belong to him.

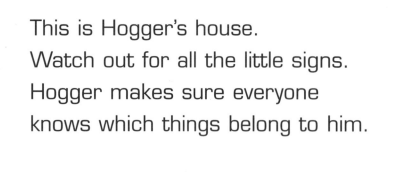

Is everyone ready?
Let's ring the door bell.

Ding Dong!

Here comes Hogger.

SSShhh…

Creeaaaaak!

The door is opening…

"SURPRISE! SURPRIIIISE!"
yells everyone.

Hogger's eyes are wide.
He doesn't say a word.

"Is he going to invite us inside?"
someone finally whispers.
"May we come in?" I ask.
"Uh, I suppose," Hogger says.
"But don't touch any of my stuff."

After we all promise, Hogger lets us inside.

Hogger watches
everyone carefully.
"Don't sit in my chairs," he tells us.
Then he whirls around.
"Don't look at my books.
Put that down, it's mine!" he shouts across the room.
Would you say that to your guests?

8

"We brought you some birthday presents," I tell him.
"And where should we put the cake?"

"Presents?" Hogger asks. "Cake? Oh, boy!" He stares at what we are carrying. "Set them down over here," he says. "Right here, next to me!" There are big boxes and small boxes. They look pretty on the table. Hogger smiles. He should say something to everyone, but he doesn't.

Hoggers Flowers No Smelling

HOGGER'S BOX -O- STUFF

Do you know what he should tell us?

Hogger grabs a big box
and starts to tear off
the wrapping paper.

"Wait!" I tell him.
"For what?" Hogger snorts.
"I want to open
presents now!
They're my presents,
aren't they?"
"Yes," I tell him.
"But we want to have
a surprise party first."

"I was surprised when I answered my door,"
Hogger says. "Now I want to open my presents.
That should be fun for everyone."

13

Just then, someone yells out,
"Let's play games."
"How about Pin-the-Wig-
on-the-Bald-Man," I suggest.
All the Beasties start
talking at once.
"We could play cards!"
"Or checkers!"
"Or video games!"
"Hogger has lots of
games in his cabinet,"
I shout over the noise.

We all love to play games. Do you?

Clump!

Bump!

Bang!

Whomp!

Hogger drops
his present.
He runs into
furniture and guests trying to get
across the room. He stands guard in front of his toy cabinet.

"Aren't you going to let us play with some of your games, Hogger?" I ask.

"No," he tells me. "No one is going to touch any of my toys! They're mine! All mine!"

Hogger doesn't like to share. Do you?

"How can we have fun if you won't let us touch your toys or your games?" I ask Hogger.

Hogger frowns. "Um… I have a new video game. You could all watch me play!"

Everyone sighs.

No one thinks that would be very much fun. Do you?

17

"Do you have a ball?" I ask Hogger.

Whomp!

He pushes the doors on the cabinet
to make sure they are closed tightly.
"Why do you want to know?" he asks.
"I thought we could play together," I tell him.
He shakes his head. "Not with my ball."

19

"Hey, look," a Beastie says loudly. "Hogger has the new Invasion of the Humanoids video!"

"We could watch that together," I say.

Hogger gasps!

His palms begin to sweat.

Stomp!

Bang!

Whoosh!

He races to the other side of the room and snatches the video away.

"This video is mine! No one else can watch it!"

"Maybe we should let him open his presents now," someone whispers. "We may as well," I agree sadly. Everyone goes over to the table, but no one is having a good time. Do you think Hogger is being nice?

Hogger sits at the end of the table. He leans forward and pulls all the presents toward himself. Then he slides the cake closer, too. "Let's start," Hogger tells us. He is smiling. Can you see any other Beasties smiling?

"Cool," Hogger says, pulling the wrapping paper off the first box. "A computer game!"

Shhriipp!

He rips open the next one.

More paper falls to the floor.

"A toy helicopter... a catcher's mitt!" Hogger yells.

Crumple!

Rip!

Shhhred!

Wrapping paper is flying in every direction.
"Ooo! A set of action figures!"
he squeals with delight.

When he finally finishes,
Hogger looks at us.
"Is this all? Aren't there
any more presents?"

24

Is Hogger making the Beasties who brought presents feel good? What should he do?

I light the birthday candles. **Whoosh!** Hogger blows them out.
Then I reach for the cake to cut it. Hogger grabs it back.

"It's mine," he insists.

"We can't have any?" I ask.

He shakes his head. "It's my birthday, so it's my cake."

"I'm not having any fun," a Beastie mumbles.

"No one is," I agree.

Are you?

Everyone gets up. They start walking toward the door.

"You can't go yet!" Hogger grunts.

"Don't you want to watch me eat my cake?"

He looks at me. "Why is everyone leaving?"

"Because you won't even
share your cake!" I tell him.

We hear the front door open.
Hogger sits still a few seconds more.
Then he jumps up. I follow him
to the door. "Wait!" Hogger calls.
Everyone stops and turns around.
"You can…" Hogger begins.

Then he frowns again.
"You can share my cake," he mutters.
"Louder," I encourage him.
"Come back and share my cake," Hogger shouts."

Everyone is amazed. They have never seen Hogger share anything. Slowly, they come back into the house.
I cut the cake. Hogger sits very still while I pass out the plates.
I am very proud of Hogger. Aren't you?

Then, everyone wants to play games again.
I can tell how hard it is for Hogger to open his toy
cabinet. We play a board game. Hogger fidgets, but I can
tell he likes having company. He counts all the game
pieces when we are done.
Uh, oh! One piece is
missing. Do you know
where it is?
Hogger starts
to get upset,
but every-
one looks
for it until
it is found.

When it is time to go home, everyone is smiling at Hogger.

"Thanks for sharing, Hogger," a Beastie calls out.

"Thanks for helping me find the missing game piece," he answers.

"This was the best birthday party I have ever had," Hogger smiles. "Maybe I could have a sleep-over next week."

"I think everyone would come," I tell him. "They had fun today." I think Hogger's parties will be a lot more fun from now on. Do you know why?